Giovanni–I enjoyed your playful conversations and curious spirit.
The memories will keep you close in my heart forever.

Kandace, Cierra, and Shadae, my adorable nieces,
thanks for your input and guidance. Love you!

To Mom and Dad and my entire family. Thank you for the traditions.
They humble me, ground me, and give me a sense of purpose.
–S.L.R.

To my Mom, the world's greatest, who once read nineteen books in a single night to an
insatiably curious little girl. Words will never adequately express my gratitude,
so I'll keep drawing pictures instead.

To Devin and Ricky–thanks for never letting me take myself too seriously;
and to the rest of my family, with whom I am so proud to share DNA. I love you all!

To all my teachers inside and outside the classroom, especially Judy Sobko, Oren Sherman,
and Margett Budinich.
–Sully

To Wendy Murphy, who is ever narrowing the six degrees of separation.
Thank you for connecting us!
–S.L.R. and Sully

ISBN 13: 978-1-940014-73-9   eISBN 13: 978-1-940014-74-6

Library of Congress Catalog Number: 2015944211
Printed in the United States of America   Second Printing: 2016
20 19 18 17 16   6 5 4 3 2

Illustrations by Megan Kayleigh Sullivan   Cover and interior design by Stephanie Bart-Horvath

Wise Ink Creative Publishing
837 Glenwood Ave.
Minneapolis, MN 55405
www.wiseinkpub.com

To order, visit www.seattlebookcompany.com or call (734) 426-6248. Reseller discounts available.

Rice & Rocks

by Sandra L. Richards

illustrated by Megan Kayleigh Sullivan

WISE Ink
CREATIVE ★ PUBLISHING

I woke up feeling great! It was Sunday. No school. No itchy uniform. I could play my trumpet, read my *Godzilla* comics, draw another frog picture, and hang out with Jasper. What I loved most about Sundays was my whole family came to visit.

Jasper is a Congo African grey parrot. He was a birthday surprise from
Auntie last year.

Everyone else thought Jasper was a normal parrot, but Auntie and I knew better.

Jasper and I were upstairs in my room when we heard a knock at the door. Then Auntie looked into my room. "May I hang out with my favorite nephew?" Auntie asked. Auntie's two dogs, Skye and Honey, followed her in.

"Auntie, what is Grandma cooking? My friends are coming over," I said.

Auntie rubbed her stomach. "She's making a traditional Sunday dish for dinner: Jamaican stewed chicken with rice and beans."

"Ugh!" I cried. "Grandma is making RICE AND ROCKS?
For my friends?"

Auntie frowned. "What's wrong, Giovanni?"

Jasper explained, "Rice and rocks is what Giovanni calls rice and beans. Have you ever noticed that he picks the rocks—I mean beans—out of the rice one at a time? When no one is looking, Giovanni gives Skye and Honey the beans under the table."

"That explains why Skye and Honey have gas on Sundays," said Auntie.

Jasper and Auntie laughed. Even the dogs grinned.

"Guys, this is not funny!" I shouted. "What if my friends don't like rice and rocks?"

Auntie hugged me. "Giovanni, having rice and beans is a family tradition tracing back to Jamaica. As a child, I loved that tradition."

"That is one old tradition if it has been around since you were a child!" Jasper joked.

"JASPER! Shut your beak. Remember, I can always return you to the pet store," Auntie teased.

"Sorry, I was just playing," Jasper apologized.

I shook my head. "C'mon, you two. This is serious! Emily, Aaron, and Gabby will be here soon. We have to break the tradition today!"

"Giovanni, do you know where your friends' families come from?" asked Auntie.

I scratched my head. "I remember Emily said her abuela, or grandmother, is from Puerto Rico. And Gabby bragged about her family playing in a band in New Orleans."

Jasper inquired, "What about Aaron?"

"Aaron's family is from Japan, home of Godzilla, king of monsters."

Auntie looked at Jasper. "Are you thinking what I'm thinking?"

"Yes, time for tradition to take flight!"

"Where are we going?" I asked.

"That's for us to know and you to find out," announced Auntie. "Grab hands, wings, and paws. Reach up, rub Jasper's beak, and close your eyes and count to five."

"One, two, three, four, five . . ."

"Open your eyes!" commanded Jasper.
   Auntie, Skye, Honey, and I were smaller than Jasper!
"Let's take a ride," Jasper insisted.

We hopped onto Jasper's back and flew out the window.

In Japan, a friend of Jasper's greeted us. Oku is a green pheasant, Japan's national bird.

"Oku, do the Japanese eat rice and rocks?" I asked.

"He means rice and beans," clarified Jasper.

Oku chuckled. "Yes, the Japanese eat rice and rocks. Sekihan, red rice boiled with red adzuki beans, is a traditional Japanese dish."

My mouth fell open. "Really? It's a tradition?"

"Sekihan is served on special occasions like birthdays and holidays. The Japanese phrase 'Let's have sekihan' means 'Let's celebrate.'"

Greetings from PUERTO RICO

In Puerto Rico we met a spindalis named Idalia. "We are the national bird," she said. "In Spanish we're called reina mora."

"Idalia, do Puerto Ricans eat rice and rocks?" I asked.

Jasper said, "He means rice and beans."

"Sí . . . I mean yes," said Idalia. "We call it arroz con gandules, rice with pigeon peas. We look forward to eating it on holidays, special occasions, and Sunday dinner.

My eyes widened. "I love Sundays," I admitted.

"Idalia!" a laughing voice called. "C'mon, you're gonna miss the start of the football game! We are saving the highest tree seat for you!"

Idalia giggled. "Okay, okay, I'm coming. Harley, for a little coquí, you have a big sound!"

"What is a coquí, Idalia?" I asked.

"A little frog," Idalia answered.

"I draw pictures of coquís all the time," I said. "Thanks, Idalia."

"De nada. You're welcome. Where are you off to next?"

Jasper replied, "N'Awlins. Otherwise known as
New Orleans, Louisiana."

STRONG

A brown pelican, the state bird of Louisiana, met us in New Orleans.

"What's up?" he said. "I'm Flint."

"I'm Giovanni," I replied. "Do people here eat rice and rocks?"

"He means rice and beans," Jasper explained.

"Do you see Louis Armstrong Park right there?" Flint pointed with his wing. "You know who Louis Armstrong is, right?"

"Louis Armstrong was only the greatest trumpet player ever! I play the trumpet, too."

"Do you know what Louis Armstrong loved to eat?" Flint quizzed.

"Don't tell me he liked rice and rocks!" I exclaimed.

Flint chuckled. "Well, if you mean red beans and rice, you are right. In fact, he signed his letters with 'Red Beans and Ricely Yours, Louis Armstrong.'"

I was amazed. "Wow, that is cool!"

Back at home, we rubbed Jasper's beak and counted to five to return to our normal size.

When my friends arrived they were hungry. We all sat down at the dining room table.

"Good evening, everyone. We are having Jamaican stewed chicken with rice and beans," announced Grandma.

"Rice and beans are my grandma's specialty," I said proudly. "On Sundays, it's a tradition in our family to eat it."

I watched my friends fill their bowls with rice and rocks.
"Mmmmmm, I love this!" said Emily. "It is just like the dish my abuela
makes, arroz con grandules! I think I'd like another serving, please.

"I have not had red beans and rice since my last visit to N'Awlins. This is really good," said Gabby, putting another spoonful in her mouth. Aaron looked confused. "Are we celebrating something?"

"We are celebrating family, friends, and traditions," I said. I grinned, glad that my friends liked rice and rocks. "It's really nice to spend time with all of you."

I love Sundays. And I am proud of our traditions.
RICE AND ROCKS ROCK!